LUCKY

LUCKY

Terry Berger

Illustrated by Darrell Wiskur

J. Philip O'Hara, Inc.
Chicago

J. Philip O'Hara, Inc. 20 East Huron, Chicago, 60611. Published simultaneously in Canada by Van Nostrand Reinhold Ltd., Scarborough, Ontario.

First Printing K

Library of Congress Number 73-16817

ISBN: 0-87955-710-9

ISBN: 0-87955-110-0

Daisy was having puppies.

And Tuffy was the reason. Tuffy was the dog next door.

Ever since we moved to the neighborhood, Tuffy had come calling. He visited old friends less and Daisy more and more.

Chasing after squirrels no longer seemed important, and he scratched at our door till someone let him in.

Inside the house, both dogs chased about. And when the attic door was open, they raced up the steps.

Daisy looked like a flying mop. She was Maltese and had silky white hair.

And Tuffy swept through the house like a broom. He was a tan and gray Yorkie.

And that's why my father was
unhappy. The puppies would be all
mixed-up. He liked things to be one
way or the other.

My mother, on the other hand, was really glad. She had the feeling that Tuffy and Daisy were really in love. And to her nothing else mattered.

I was feeling good and bad about it, but my brother David was mad. He said there were plenty of dogs in the world already, and he was against us making more.

Daisy, herself, enjoyed being pregnant for she was fed and petted all day.

Her belly hung so low it brushed against the carpet. And my hand across her bottom could feel a puppy's kick.

Sometimes Tuffy's whole family stopped in to see her. And friends and neighbors came by to watch her grow.

Then, two weeks before the puppies came, we made a special bed. It was time to prepare for that day.

Mother bought cans of milk in case Daisy couldn't nurse. And I found tiny bottles to put it in.

Our vet said the rest was up to Daisy. And he was sure she'd know what to do.

But not one of us really believed him, for Daisy had not learned to *sit* on command. That she knew about babies seemed doubtful.

The night before we expected her to, Daisy gave birth. She went straight to her bed like she was supposed to.

Nervously I watched her panting and pressing, and in my mind I counted out puppies. One for grandpa, one for Tuffy's folks, and please, please, one for us.

And then I sat and thought about Daisy and just how much I loved her.

And I prayed nothing bad would hap-
pen.

With the first puppy about to come, someone rang the doorbell. Daisy reared up and barked and I clutched at my brother's arm. It was hard to believe she was thinking of us now.

Another squeeze and the first pup
was out. It came in a little bag.

Biting the bag, Daisy tore it open and the puppy began to breathe.

23

Then, taking the cord that had carried its food, Daisy chewed it off and ate it up.

Next she licked the puppy clean and pushed it around to dry it.

Hearing a tiny cry, we knew that all was well.

A half hour later, Daisy pressed
down again and the second pup came
out. It came in another bag.

Quickly biting the bag, Daisy tore
it open so this pup could breathe too.

Then she chewed the second cord
off at the navel and ate that one up
too.

Licking the second puppy clean, she pushed it around to dry it.

She pushed it around again and again, but there was no tiny cry.

It took a long time for all of us to agree that the second pup was dead. And then I cried.

Daisy had no time for sorrow and went back to licking her first pup. She helped it to suck on her nipple, knowing he needed her now.

There were no other puppies. While Daisy cared for her first, we tearfully buried the second. The second was larger and prettier, but the first one looked like Tuffy.

And we knew that he would be proud!

David said because there was only one puppy Daisy could give it more attention. I felt good about Daisy being all right, but bad about the other puppy dying.

That night we all realized what life meant to us—even the life of a pup.

We found that out and I guess we're lucky.

And to help us remember, we kept
Daisy's pup. We kept him and we
call him Lucky.

TERRY BERGER, as you may have suspected, is the owner of Daisy and Lucky—and the story is a true one. Besides being a dog owner and a mother, Ms. Berger writes other books that deal with children's feelings on their own level. The simple truth and beauty required in writing for children is a constant challenge to her.

DARRELL WISKUR's avid interest in photography and nature study is an important factor in the many assignments he receives to illustrate animal stories. He is also keenly interested in Bible study and game design. Darrell and his wife, Patricia, live outside Chicago with their six children.

This book was set in 18 point Linofilm Times Roman.